The Perfect Pet

By Gracie & Emma VanDonkersgoed

I think I'd like an elephant

But he would be too big.

Such a pet would be so fun

If it could dance a jig!

I think I'd like a spider

But that just would not do.

My mom would be so mad

She'd hit it with her shoe!

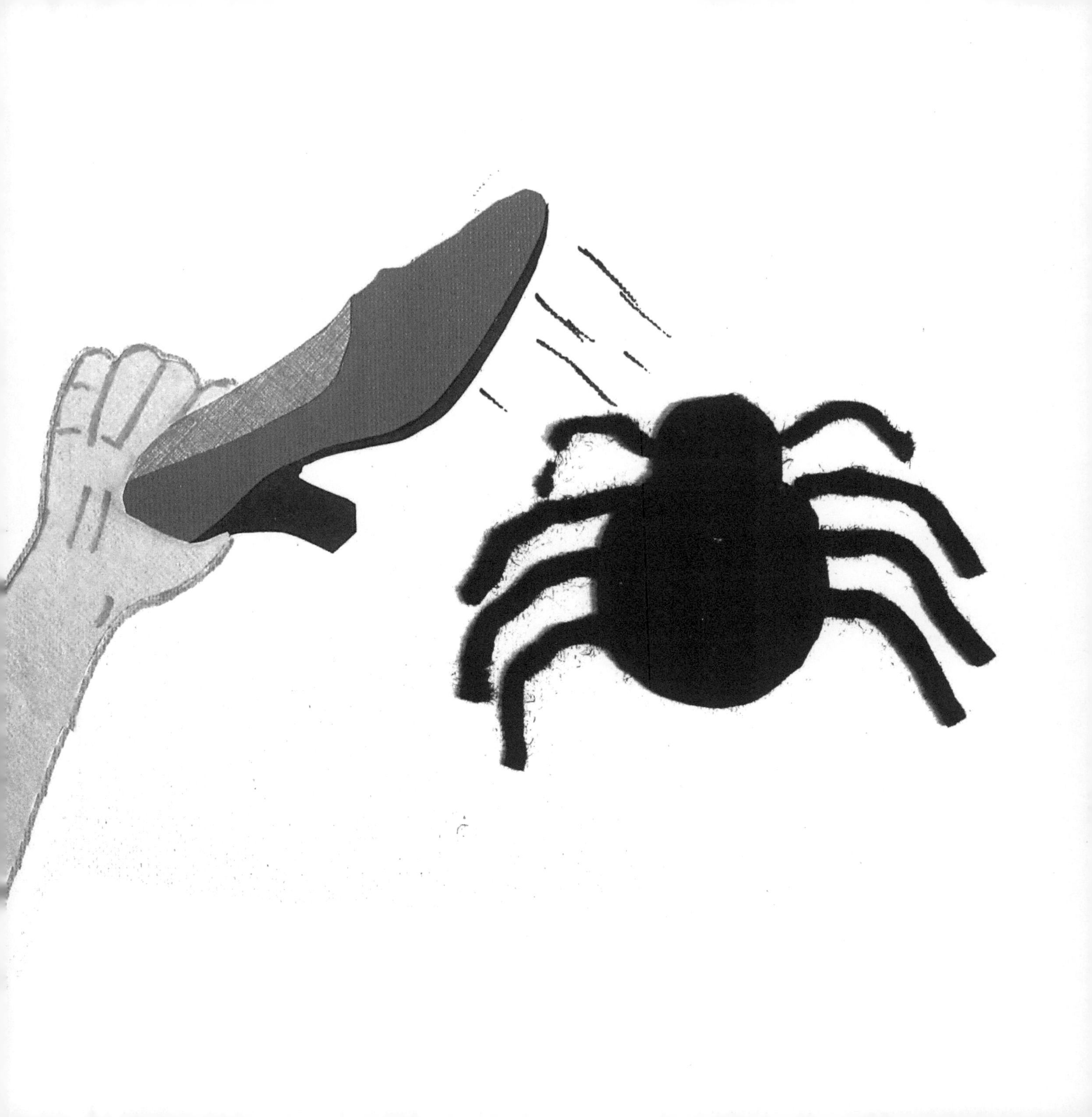

I think I'd like a small giraffe
But they are oh so tall.
Wouldn't it look funny
Trying to catch a ball!

I think I’d like to choose an owl
But he’d keep me up all night.
So many choices for a pet
And I have to get it right!

I think I'd like a dolphin
To splash with in the sea.
But if I'm being honest
It shouldn't live with me!

I think I'd like a dragon
But they're so hard to get.
And putting out their smoke and fire
Would leave us all so wet!

I think I'd like a squirrel
For they're so cute and small.
But Dad would say NO so loud
It would disappear till fall!

NO

I think I'd like a tiger
But it would be too wild.
I need to have a smaller pet
One that's much more mild.

I think I'd like to have a snake
But feeding would be a chore.
I only have one sister
And it would want much more!

I think I'd like a porcupine
It would be so unique.
But it would be so spikey
I'd never get to sleep!

I think I'd like a parrot

But it would talk all day.

I'd throw him out the window

And send him on his way!

Hello!
Good bye!
come in!
Go out!

I think I’d like a fish

But cuddling would be so tricky.

His skin is very slimy

And really oh so icky!

I think I’d like a goat
To play with in the yard
But keeping him in line
Would just be too hard.

I think I'd like a bear
For they're so big and great.
But it is far too hairy
I think I'll have to wait.

CPSIA information can be obtained
at www.ICGtesting.com
Printed in the USA
LVHW050400220619
622024LV00002B/9/P